Pat and the Magic Hat

Colin and Jacqui Hawkins

FAMILY LEARNING

FAMILY LEARNING

from Dorling Kindersley

*The Family Learning mission is to support the concept
of the home as a centre of learning and to help families
develop independent learning skills to last a lifetime.*

Editors: Bridget Gibbs, Fiona Munro
Designers: Chris Fraser, Claire Ricketts

Published by Family Learning

Dorling Kindersley registered offices:
9 Henrietta Street, Covent Garden, London WC2E 8PS

VISIT US ON THE WORLD WIDE WEB AT:
http://www.dk.com

ISBN 0-7513-7173-4

Colour reproduction by DOT Gradations
Printed in Hong Kong by Wing King Tong

A CIP catalogue record for this book is
available from the British Library.

Pat the cat needs a new hat.

There's a knock at the door,
RAT-A-TAT-TAT!
"Who is that?" said Pat the cat.

It was Nat the rat
with a parcel for Pat.
"A box for me!
What can it be?"
said Pat the cat to
Nat the rat.

"This letter's from Mig,
the pig with the wig,"
said Nat to Pat.
"It's a magic hat, Pat!"
"A magic hat, Nat?
Can it really be that?" said Pat.
"Yes it is," said Nat.
"You must wear this hat to go
on Mig the pig's TV show."

Magic? Do you think so?

Give it a go!

It's from Mig, the superstar pig.

Dear Pat,
Please wear this magic hat
on my show.   Love, Mig.
            x

"Come on, hat," said Nat.
"Make some magic
for Pat!" KERZAP!
With a loud thunderclap,
the magic hat
became a cap.

"That's nice and flat, and it flatters you, Pat," said Nat.
"No, Nat," said Pat.
"Flat caps make me look fat."
"You're right, Pat, that cap looks natty, but you are a fatty."

"It doesn't look right.
It should have more height!"
said Pat. KERPLAT!
The hat became tall
and not flat at all.

"Well, look at that, Pat," said Nat.
"Now it's a tall hat."
"But Nat," said Pat, "it's a
pointy hat. I don't like
pointy hats. It should be
less pointy than that."

That's
a tall hat,
Pat.

A hat
for a dunce?
Change it
at once!

"Nat, this hat is too big for me.
I just can't see."
"Well, Pat, that's true, of course,"
said Nat to Pat,
"and you don't have a horse."
"Magic hat, please can you
change into something less
strange?" said Pat to the hat.

With a SPLIT! and a SPLAT!
Pat's cowcat hat
became a seacat hat.
"Why Captain Pat," said Nat,
"that is a great hat, a heave-ho
and off-we-go sort of hat."

"No! Silly Nat, I don't like that," said Pat. "I don't have a boat and cats don't float. I'm not that sort of pet, and water's very wet."

"Oh my! Oh my!" said Nat with a sigh. "Magic hat, can you try to be a hat that keeps Pat dry?"

SPLISH! SPLASH! SPLAT!
Captain Pat's seacat hat
was now a super swim hat!
"Pat, that's the very thing.
And you've got a rubber ring!"
said Nat to Pat.
"How do you like that?"

Pat's in the swim.

Look at him!

"I've had enough
of this magic stuff,"
said Pat to Nat.
"A smart new hat is all I need."
"Yes indeed," Nat agreed.

KERZAT!
The magic hat changed for Pat.

"That's the hat,"
said Pat to Nat.
"In this hat I will go far,
I'll become a superstar."

Pat then saw
a magic wand was in his paw!
"Now," said Nat, "off you go
to Mig the pig's big TV show."
With magic wand and magic
hat, Pat was now a magic cat.